HER LIGHT CHASE

SCION SERIES, CHASE WALKER

L.P. DILLON

CHAPTER

One

With a beaming smile on my face, my mind raced as I drove us towards our surprise date. My proposal to Aubrey wasn't exactly special. We'd had an Alpha sniffing around in the woods, and Aubrey had asked me to turn her. She didn't want her family or my pack having to protect her any longer. She wanted to be strong in her own right. That's when I explained that we'd have to get married before I could turn her. With a little more hesitation than I felt comfortable with, she agreed. I wanted to make tonight perfect, by proposing to her properly and romantically. She deserved a night that she'd never forget. One she'd be proud to tell our children and grandchildren about. I wanted to show her exactly how much she meant to me and that she was my one, my only, my everything.

To be honest, I still couldn't believe that the most incredible

Scion had strolled right into my life, and she was about to become my wife. Aubrey and I had known each other only a short while, but in that time, she had become my entire world. I couldn't imagine myself with anyone else. I wished I could say that she felt the same way.

My smile gradually faded.

"So, I was thinking of Paris for our honeymoon?" I questioned Aubrey with a side glance, hopeful that I'd made the right suggestion.

She didn't bother to look at me when she replied, "um-hm."

I turned my attention back to the road ahead, gripping hold of the steering wheel a little tighter.

"Or maybe somewhere else in Europe? I know you loved the idea of going there ..."

"Ah-huh," she mumbled.

She clearly wasn't paying the slightest bit of attention to what I was saying.

"Or we can go somewhere hotter, like Hawaii or something?"

"Yeah, sounds good."

Fuck this!

"Or maybe we'll just fly to the moon?" I growled, hoping it would snap her out of her daydream. It didn't.

"Yeah, that would be perfect," she replied while continuing to stare out of the car window.

"Aubrey!" I snapped, quickly pulling a "huh?" from her lips.

"Are you even listening to me? I'm trying to plan our honeymoon here, and you're acting like you don't give a shit. What gives?"

"Nothing. I'm sorry. I guess I'm just a little distracted."

No shit. She's been like this for weeks. I can't take it anymore.

"A little? Are you kidding me? It's like you're not even here anymore. I'm pretty much planning this whole wedding with Payton and your mother," I yelled, then paused as I skidded the car to a stop at the side of the road.

She flew forward then slammed back into her seat. Usually, I would have felt guilty for hurting her, but at this precise moment, I was beyond angry. She stared at me while I gripped the steering wheel tight enough to make my knuckles turn white. I took in a deep breath, and eventually exhaled it, trying my best to calm myself.

"Look, if you don't want to do this, I understand. We can call it all off," I virtually whispered while twisting my hands around the steering wheel.

I don't want her to call it off, and I certainly don't understand. How can she still be in love with him? He's gone, and he's never coming back. Fuck!

"I don't understand. Of course, I don't want you to call it off. I love you ..." She replied as she leaned forward and cupped my chin with her hand.

I wanted to believe her, I really did, but she had been so distant lately, I knew something wasn't right. She tried to turn my head to look at her, but I knew as soon as my eyes met those beautiful blue pools, I'd be putty in her hands. I loved the girl more than I'd ever thought was possible. No one came close to her.

The day she crashed into my life, flying panties and dildo in tow, I knew she was the one. I couldn't explain it. I'd never told a

3

girl that I loved them before, but the moment I looked into her gorgeous eyes I wanted to blurt the words out right then and there.

I pushed her hands away and averted my gaze, *you need to be strong, Chase.*

That didn't last long. The AC picked up her delicious scent and floated it right under my nose, as if trying to tease me. Taking in her hypnotic smell, I couldn't help but look at her. It was like she had strings controlling every inch of me. I spoke softly to her, the whole situation was breaking my heart, and I couldn't bear it any longer.

"I love you too. More than you can possibly imagine. I've loved you since the first day you arrived here and slammed into me with your box of underwear. Hell, even seeing you blush after I tripped over your vibrator made me love you even more. But I'm not convinced this is what you really want, that I'm *who* you want."

It's about time she knew. I know what she truly feels, and who she is in love with, and it's not me.

She placed her hand over her face, closed her eyes, and sighed.

"Of course I want you. I want this, want a future with you. I love you, Chase."

"You love Jesse!" I growled.

I couldn't help how it came out, admitting it out loud absolutely crushed me. I loved her more than I loved myself, more than I loved anyone or anything in this world, but she still loved him.

Her hand fell from her face and her eyes sprung open in shock, "What?"

"You heard me. You dream about him all the damn time, and you call out his name while you sleep. Even when you're with me, you're not really there. You're off in some dreamland with him, aren't you?" I had to keep my voice low, if I lost control right now, I wasn't sure how far I'd take it.

She sat in front of me and just stared into my eyes, not saying a damn word, while my heart broke in front of her. After a few minutes, I closed my eyes and sighed, turning the car around to take her back to the Sorority house. I drove in silence, and she did nothing to ease the tension. It was clear to me that she wasn't going to fight for me, for us.

It hurts so damn much. I'm losing her ... no ... how can I lose someone that was never mine, to begin with? Her heart was always his.

I had no choice but to go ahead with my dad's plan. There was no way I could marry Aubrey knowing that she would never love me the way she loved my cousin.

I've got no choice. I've got to leave her. I'm not strong enough to stay ... I really wish I was.

I pulled up outside the Sorority house. I could tell she was waiting for me to get out of the car, but I wasn't going to. I couldn't; my legs felt like jelly. I just sat there gripping the steering wheel again, staring straight ahead.

"Get out, Aubrey," my voice sounded defeated.

"What? Aren't you coming in? We need to talk about this ..."

"No, we don't. It's simple, we're done, it's over ..."

5

The words cut through my heart, and it took all I had to keep my emotions in check.

She grabbed my arm and cried out, "What? No, it's not. Chase, look at me!"

I pushed her hand off my arm and turned my head away from her, I didn't want her to see the tear that had escaped my eye and was now crawling down my cheek.

"Chase, please don't do this. Look at me. Please, Chase, I love you. We can work through this ..." She begged.

I couldn't answer her— if I did, I was sure the words would come out shaky, instantly allowing her to talk me 'round. I needed to stay strong.

Slowly, I got out of the car, and with carefully placed steps I moved to her door and opened it.

"Please get out of the car, Aubrey. I need to leave ..."

She did as she was asked and got out of the car, but she didn't stand still. Instead, she threw her arms around me. I didn't return the hug but stood rigid with my arms hanging at my sides. I wanted to melt into her embrace, but I felt betrayed, hurt, crushed. Tears stained her cheeks, and when she angled her head to look at me, I started crying too.

I couldn't remember the last time I'd cried. I had never been one to let the softer side of me out. I was a future Alpha; I couldn't look weak. I took in a deep breath through my nose, pulling back the tears, the pain, and shoving them as far down as I could.

"Chase, please don't leave," she begged, her voice as broken as my heart.

"Aubrey, I have to ... my heart is breaking, and I can't keep competing with a dead man," my voice cracked a little as I wiggled out of her grip. Her amazingly soft and warm embrace, one I wasn't sure I'd ever feel again.

With those words said, I turned and walked towards the driver's side of the car. After one last agonizing gaze at her, I got inside my car, closed the door, and sped off. That was the moment I'd left my heart in Murston. I was now alone, broken, and surrounded by eternal emptiness. I had no one else to blame, it was *HIS* fault.

CHAPTER
Two

"If he wasn't already dead, I'd find the son of a bitch and kill him myself ..." I bellowed while standing from the couch, grabbing hold of the coffee table, and effortlessly launching it into the air. My dad watched; his face unchanging as the table smashed into the wall.

"Fuck!"

My fists were clenched tighter than I'd ever thought possible. If they got any tighter, I was sure I'd break every tiny bone inside them.

"Son, you need to calm down. She isn't worth your anger, or your pain. There are more Scions in the world," his voice was deep and commanding.

"I don't want another Scion. I want Aubrey!" I yelled at him, then slumped back onto the couch. "Dad, I know you hate her, but can't you understand? I'm completely in love with the girl."

I fell forward, covering my face with my hands. I needed to breathe, keep my emotions in check. There was no way in hell I could let my father see me cry. It took me years to convince him that I was strong enough to challenge Jesse for the Alpha position. If he thought Aubrey had made me soft, there would be no chance in hell that he'd accept her.

Not that it matters now.

I felt the couch sink beside me as my father took a seat. Draping his arm over my shoulders he pulled my head into his chest.

"Son, you need to let her go. She was never meant to be yours."

I wanted to argue with him. Convince him that she was my one. But I couldn't. I knew he was right. Deep down I hoped that in time she could love me the same way she loved Jesse, but I didn't have the strength to wait. I couldn't spend my life watching her pine after my dead cousin.

Every time we got close; would she be wishing I was him? I couldn't live with that paranoia, that constant pain and jealousy. Leaving her broke my heart, but I knew that staying would kill me.

"So, what now? The proposal... Shit. The wedding?" I pulled away from my dad and slumped back onto the couch again.

"Don't worry about all that. Your mother is sending everyone cancellation emails now. She's trying to busy herself. She doesn't know how to fix this, and you know how she likes to fix things."

A slight smile reached my lips. I was lucky to have my parents; they did everything they could to protect and support me. I glanced up at my father. "Look, I know the timing isn't perfect, but we can still put my plan into action."

I turned away from him in thought. He came to me months ago with his plan, when Aubrey wasn't responding to my advances. He told me that an acquaintance of his had reached out for help. It was the Alpha from the Soulcrest pack. He was getting older, and he needed a future Alpha for his Scion daughter.

When my father came to me with the plan, I stopped him in his tracks, I wasn't interested. Aubrey was already the focus of all my attention. I knew Jesse had been sniffing around, but that didn't bother me. The day he gave up the future Alpha position, was the day that he lost all claims to any Scions that crossed into our territory.

If things had been different, Aubrey would have been off-limits for me. I would have focused on finding a werewolf girl to settle with, like Cassidy. But I was an Alpha— it was my responsibility to find a Scion and carry on my family bloodline. The moment I saw Aubrey, I knew I had found my one, so my father's plan wasn't of interest.

"So, what was the plan?" I asked in hushed curiosity.

I didn't want anyone else, I wanted Aubrey, but she didn't want me, and I still had a duty to my pack. *Maybe I could learn to love this new Scion?*

"Okay, so Charles and Theia Stonefeather were only blessed with one child. A daughter named Olivia," he explained.

Nice name.

"She has been reluctant to find an Alpha. Her parents don't understand why she is stalling, but every time they bring up the subject, she throws a hissy fit."

Oh great, a drama queen, I thought with an eye roll. The last thing I needed right now was another high maintenance woman in my life. But I couldn't go back to Aubrey, I just couldn't.

"Anyway, Charles is fed up with negotiating with his daughter. He feels it's about time that she sucked it up and put her pack first. Now, I know this means you'll have to challenge her father for his Alpha position, once you defeat your uncle, but this is a chance to make our pack the largest in the country."

I glanced up at him, his face was lit up with excitement. I replied with my own soft smile. I didn't want to do this in the slightest, but I couldn't lie, the idea of ruling over the largest pack in the country did sound impressive. If I couldn't have Aubrey, then at least I could go down in history as the greatest Alpha, ever.

"Okay, tell me everything," I demanded, pulling a smug grin from my father's face.

We talked for a few hours, he told me everything I needed to know about the plan and Olivia's pack. To be honest, having something else to focus on helped a lot. The more I thought about the merging of our packs, the less I thought about my broken heart. If I kept it as a business transaction, stayed disconnected, strong and focused, then I would be able to make it through.

This was the best thing for me and my pack. Aubrey had made it clear who she wanted, and although he wasn't ever coming back, I didn't deserve to be second best. I'd feel like she only settled for me because she couldn't have him, and I was worth more than that.

Sure, I'd made mistakes in my life. I'd made the wrong choices, slept around, and hurt people, but it was time for me to grow up. Time to take control of my life, quit being so selfish, and become the Alpha that my pack deserved. My first step, get myself a Scion.

"So, when do we leave?" I asked my father once we'd finished discussing all the details.

"First thing in the morning. I'll call Charles now and set up a meeting." He stood from the couch, pulled his phone out of his pocket, and began to walk away. "Son?"

"Yeah?" I replied, glancing over at him.

"This really is the best thing for our family and the pack. I'm so proud of you." He gave me a small smile, then walked away, "Charlie. Hi, I have great news..."

I got off of the couch and headed up the stairs and toward my old room. Arabella and I stayed over occasionally, so our rooms were kept how we liked them. I made my way into my room and headed into the bathroom for a shower. Once showered and changed, I jumped into my bed. As soon as my eyes closed, pictures of Aubrey flooded every inch of the darkness.

I could hear my phone vibrating on the nightstand beside me. I sighed while opening my eyes, reached over to the bedside table and picked up my phone. There were dozens of missed calls and texts from Aubrey, Arabella, Bear, and even Payton. I deleted all of them, I didn't want to talk, to explain what happened, I just wanted to forget about Brie for a while.

I scrolled down to Connor's text. It was just him asking if I was okay. I replied, letting him know that I was going ahead with my father's plan and that I would be radio silent for a while. He texted back asking what he should do about Aubrey. I just replied *'Nothing'*.

I knew that once I was gone, my uncle wouldn't sign off on extra protection from the pack. If she wasn't a future mate of mine, she didn't matter to the pack in his eyes. The thought scared me, knowing that without the protection of the pack, a Sire, King, or Alpha could easily get to her. As much as that thought killed me, this was her choice; her decision. She didn't want my pack protecting her anyway. She had no one to blame but *herself!*

CHAPTER
Three

We were in my dad's car heading towards the Soulcrest pack. I'd asked my dad to stop off at a mall on the way so I could buy a new phone. Aubrey and Bella had been blowing mine up all night, so the thing went for a swim in the toilet. I needed to focus on the plan. It was about time I started acting like an Alpha, not a lovesick teenager.

I'd bought a new cell and texted Connor. He was the only one I could trust with anything. Arabella made it clear that her loyalty lay with Aubrey. I understood, it was the way of the werewolf sorority. Werewolf girls needed to stick together. When any of them went into heat, it was brutal. Male werewolves from miles around became aggressive and fights broke out regularly.

The sorority was set up many generations ago. It was a safe haven for all un-bonded she-wolves in the territory. They all stuck together and had plans in place to hide away the she-wolves while they went through their heat. Without complete trust and loyalty, the system wouldn't work.

In the old days, when a she-wolf went into heat, male were-wolves would compete with each other, the winner taking the girl for himself and marking her. The poor girl didn't have much choice who she ended up with. So, I completely understood her reasoning. She didn't want to let her sisters down, but that meant that I couldn't trust her to have my best interests at heart.

I let Connor know that I was heading out of town, and I would contact him when I'd be returning. I didn't know how long I'd be away for, but I would keep him posted. I placed my phone back in my pocket and sighed. I knew the plan, knew what I had to do, and I was ready.

We finally pulled off the main road and onto a private drive. Once we were outside the giant house, we all got out of the car. Standing at the door ready to greet us was a large man with dark hair. I could smell that he was an Alpha. Beside him stood a small blonde-haired woman. I guessed they were Olivia's parents.

My mom and dad walked ahead and greeted the pair. It was all pleasant handshakes and hugs, and when they were finished greeting each other, they all turned their attention to me.

Well, that's fucking creepy, I thought while they all stood there staring at me with cheesy grins on their faces. I awkwardly cleared my throat and held my hand out for Alpha Stonefeather to shake.

"It's a pleasure to meet you, Alpha Stonefeather."

He smiled widely at me and as he shook my hand, he pulled me into a hug. With a chuckle he said,

"You're virtually family. Call me Charlie."

My face was squashed up against his chest. The guy was surprisingly solid for his age. Our culture was a strange one. By the time I got used to this guy, built up some sort of relationship, it would be time to fight him to the death. I didn't understand how old traditions like this were allowed to continue in this day and age, but it was what it was.

After a rough pat on my back, he finally let me go. He held onto my shoulders and pushed me away from him slightly. After a quick scan down and back up, he smiled and patted my shoulder, before turning away and ushering my father into the house. I kinda felt like a piece of meat, or a second-hand car being given the once over, but it was the way of some packs.

Not all packs allowed their Scion daughters the chance at a normal human childhood. Most Scions knew exactly what they were and what was expected of them. A lot of packs, tribes, and broods still had arranged marriages. It was pretty barbaric really. Basically, the Scion went to whoever offered the father the most.

Luckily for Olivia, her parents cared somewhat about who they wanted for their daughter. They were a wealthy oil industry pack from what my father had told me, so money wasn't of concern for them. Our family made our money in property development, so money wouldn't have been an issue if we needed it as an offering.

Charles and Theia were more interested in making sure their daughter married an Alpha. They didn't like the idea of her marrying another type of shifter. Some leaders didn't care. Money and power drove their decisions. For Olivia's family, it was important to keep their bloodline pure. That was a concern for my family too, they wanted a werewolf Scion for me.

After greeting Theia, I was escorted into the house. It was very grand and beautiful. They had maids and pack members everywhere, but after an hour of pleasantries, there was still no sign of Olivia. I knew this was an arranged marriage, but I still needed to see the woman I would be spending the rest of my life with.

I was trying to change and do the right thing for my pack, but I was pretty shallow as a person. Some people say that it's the personality that counts, and I agree somewhat. You can be attracted to someone's personality, but I'll be honest, you still need some sort of physical attraction, or at least I do.

I sat there picturing what she would look like, but all my mind could picture was Aubrey. I sighed and stared off into space as my parents and the Stonefeathers worked out all the details and plans for my and Olivia's marriage. I couldn't help it, but my heart was hurting so much, all I really wanted was Aubrey, she was the only person I could picture myself with.

Then there she was. Her scent hit my nose, long before my eyes met hers. She was nervously standing by the door, twirling a curl of her golden blonde hair around her finger. When her eyes met mine, her cheeks blushed. I couldn't deny the girl was an absolute stunner. *Maybe this could work?* I thought while clearing my throat.

"Ah, Olivia. Nice of you to finally grace us with your presence," her father said while standing and ushering her over to us.

I swept my hand through my hair expecting her to blush again, but she didn't. Out of the corner of my eye, I saw a woman slinking towards the front door. She was a beautiful mixed-race woman, with dark hair that was dyed purple at the ends. It swept over to the side and loose curls framed her face, while the other side was shaved short.

When I sniffed the air, I could tell she was a rare human shifter. She glanced over toward Olivia and smiled sweetly, and while her cheeks blushed, it dawned on me that she was the reason why Olivia was so flustered. They were an item. I was sure of it. I'd seen that look many times before, it was one of love and adoration.

The woman noticed me staring, and no sooner had her eyes met mine, she pulled the door open and hurried out. As soon as the door clicked, Olivia cleared her throat and confidently made her way over to her parents. She kissed her father and mother, then sat down beside her mom on the couch. Her parents hadn't noticed the woman leaving and continued to chat away with my mom and dad, and after a while they excused themselves, saying they had business to discuss and that Olivia and I needed time to get acquainted.

I watched silently as my parents left the room, followed by Charles and Theia. Olivia escorted them to the door and gently closed it behind them. I casually stretched my arms across the back of the couch and rested one of my legs on top of the other.

This should be good, I thought as I prepared myself for whatever bullshit Olivia was going to spin me.

She sighed while facing the door. I was expecting her to play along with the shenanigans, but she didn't. She spun around, placed her hands on her hips, and began to ramble.

"Right, I'm just gonna lay it on the line. I'm not interested in you. I will never be interested in you. So, you might as well just tell your parents that it didn't work out. We don't get along, and I'm not the girl for you. Got it?"

My brow raised, and I couldn't help it, her little speech and the dominance she tried to show was adorable and beyond comical. I burst out laughing, and when her face twisted into a look of pure anger, I folded over as my laughter hit an all-new high. I could hear her gasp in shock, and I guessed I looked pretty silly to her, but I couldn't believe what was happening.

I had spent the last few days convincing myself that I needed to let Aubrey go, needed to move on, and now, well, now that didn't look like it was going to happen. I couldn't help but wonder if it was a weird twist of fate. Olivia was clearly in a relationship with that shifter, and there was me thinking that she was going to be the one to help me get over Aubrey. I guess the universe had other plans.

CHAPTER
Four

O nce my laughter ceased, I glanced up at Olivia. She
stood in front of me with her hands on her hips
and a completely unimpressed look on her face. I sat
upright and composed myself.

"What's so damn funny?" She snapped at me, and I found it
hard not to chuckle again.

I decided to wind her up — I couldn't help it, she looked like
such a cute little angry woman.

"What if I don't want to?"

"Huh?" She asked in confusion.

I stood up and strolled towards her. I slipped my hand
around her waist, resting it on the small of her back, before
yanking her body close to mine. With my other hand, I swept her
long blonde hair behind her ear as I leaned in. As my breath

brushed against her cheek, I could hear her heart speeding up, her breathing became labored, and I knew she was attracted to me on some level.

I made sure my voice was low and smooth as I said,

"What if I say no? What reason could you possibly have to reject me?"

"I ... Um ..." She stuttered.

"Unless you can give me a valid reason as to why I should call this whole thing off, I can't see why I shouldn't mark you right here, right now ..." I whispered in a husky tone as I moved my lips closer to her skin. "I know you're attracted to me. Your body is screaming out for me to bite you."

"No! ... No, it's not ... Mmmm," her protests quickly turned into a delicious moan when my lips met the delicate spot of flesh between her neck and her shoulder. As a Scion, she was instinctively attracted to future or current Alphas, Sires, and Kings. It was her body's way of making sure only the best would father her children.

In all honesty, I was being an asshole, taking advantage of her body's natural instincts. If I was going to let my father and pack down, and hers, I needed a very good reason to. Not just because she demanded it. I also doubted that she would openly tell me that she was in a relationship with that shifter, so I needed a way of coaxing it out of her. Also, I won't lie, it was fun to tease her a little. My bad-boy antics had all but ceased lately, and it was exciting to play the role again, even if it was only for a short while.

"Well, if there is nothing to stop me, I guess I'll just give your body what it wants."

I opened my mouth, making her body shudder as my lips brushed against her skin. I extended my canines and as they scraped along her flesh I began to panic, *shit, is she not gonna stop me? Crap!* I tilted my head back as my canines extended to their fullest, by now my wolf instinct had taken over and I couldn't stop myself.

I let out a growl as I threw my head forward, ready to plunge my teeth into her neck. With my eyes closed, I didn't see her fist flying toward my face. It cracked me in the side of the head, making me lose my footing and crash to the floor.

"Shit, why'd you do that?"

"Why do you think?! You were gonna mark me, you son of a bitch!" She growled while giving me a swift kick to the gut.

As I exhaled heavily, I couldn't help but begin to chuckle again.

"Now why are you laughing? Do you need me to kick the crap out of you, you damn creep?" She pulled her leg back ready to kick me again, and as funny as the situation was, I didn't like where her foot was aimed.

I quickly covered my crown jewels with one hand and waved the other in the air,

"No. No stop. It was a joke, I swear."

She lowered her foot to the ground and with a little stamp replied,

"A joke?! Well, forgive me for not seeing the funny side of you marking me against my wishes."

She was angry and she had every right to be. If I was in her position, I guess I wouldn't have been pleased either. "Christ, what sort of pack are you from? My father said you were from a respectful and caring pack. I guess he got that completely wrong," she mumbled as she made her way over to the couch.

I dragged myself off the floor while she took a seat. Rubbing my jaw, I replied,

"No, he didn't. We are a good pack, and I'm not all that bad, I promise."

"Then why pull a stunt like that? You were acting like a damn Neanderthal."

"I was just playing. I wanted to know if what I saw was correct," I explained while sitting down on the couch opposite her.

With a confused expression, she asked,

"What did you see?"

"You, being in love with that human shifter."

"Shhh!" She protested in a panic as she rushed over towards me. "Please, don't let them hear you," she begged while roughly grabbing my face.

I sat there in shock and just nodded in agreement. She let out a sigh of relief then slumped back onto the couch. "I knew today was a bad idea. We always say that we're gonna control ourselves, but it never works out. I can't believe we were so stupid." She sat back up and gazed into my eyes, I could see tears filling up her own. "Please, I'm begging you, don't tell anyone. My father will kill us."

The sadness in her face threw me. She really loved the shifter, and I couldn't understand why her father wouldn't let the pair of them be together.

"I won't, I swear. But why can't you be together? I know your father wants you to be with an Alpha, but surely if you're in love, he can make an exception for a King?"

She sighed again.

"If only it were that simple. She isn't a King, or Queen for that matter. She is just a normal tribe member." She sat back and covered her face. "It's such a mess. We've loved each other for years. I have tried everything I could to put off meeting any of the future mates my father had picked out for me. And I've tried everything to pave the way to coming out to him, and explaining what, and who I want, but he's so traditional and set in his ways."

"I'm so sorry Olivia, I had no idea."

"It's okay, you weren't supposed to know. I'm just sorry you've had a wasted journey."

I sat back against the couch and turned my head to face her.

"Maybe I haven't." She turned her head and glanced at me with a questioning look. "Maybe I can help you."

She sat up, giving me her full attention.

"How?"

"Maybe we can come up with a plan that benefits us both? My family will get off my back for a while, and you can finally be with your shifter."

"Claudia," she stated. "I'm listening. What do you have in mind?"

"Maybe we should discuss this somewhere away from our parents?"

"Oh. Agreed."

We had dinner with our parents, and afterwards, we told

them that we needed to get to know each other better. Olivia told them that she was going to be showing me the nightlife around town. Our parents didn't suspect a thing and actually seemed excited for us. Little did they know, we'd soon be playing them all.

We got ready as if we were going dancing, and I have to say Olivia looked amazing. If this wasn't all a lie, she would definitely be someone I could see myself with. She stashed a bag in her car which had a spare set of clothes and pajamas for us both. We were going to be calling her father later and letting him know that we were too drunk to come home and that we'd be staying at a hotel.

We said our goodbyes and headed off to the hotel. We had already booked a room and Claudia would be meeting us there. I had a few ideas about how to help them, and to be honest, it would help me in the long run. My dad would back off and leave me to it, thinking I was courting Olivia. I still loved Aubrey. Being away from her was hurting more and more with every passing hour.

Having Olivia and Claudia to focus on helped me keep her out of my thoughts for a while. Maybe bringing two people together would calm my broken heart a little. I didn't know what the future held, but I knew I'd do everything I could to make sure these two women could build a future together. Love should always come first. I just wished that Aubrey wanted me enough to risk it all.

25

CHAPTER
Five

All three of us had changed into our pajamas. If someone walked in right now, I'm sure they'd assume we were some sort of throuple. Olivia had booked the penthouse suite, so we had two bedrooms, a living room, a little kitchen, and two bathrooms. I swear it was bigger than most people's apartments. Not that I was complaining. We ordered Chinese take-out and sat down to discuss their lives and my plan.

They told me about how they met, how they fell in love, and although it warmed my heart, it made me miss Aubrey even more. I sat there noticing every little giggle or look that they gave each other, every delicate touch, they were so in love. I tried to remember if Aubrey ever acted like that with me, and I couldn't remember a single time.

She'd never looked at me like that, sure she'd blush or bite her lip, but that was more sexual chemistry. What these guys had was pure love. While Claudia and Olivia were chatting, I stood up and made my way toward the kitchen. I opened the fridge and took out a bottle of beer. Popping it open with the bottle opener, I sighed and took a large gulp.

"Chase, you okay?" Olivia's dark brown eyes searched mine, while her voice was laced with concern. A soft brush of her fingers on my arm, made me feel warm and loved. The girl really was the sweetest.

With a fake smile, I replied, "Yeah, I'm fine."

"Now that's a load of horse shit," Claudia said sarcastically before pulling the fridge door open and disappearing behind it.

"Claudia!" Olivia snapped.

"Well, it is. There is clearly something wrong with him, and I thought tonight was about complete honesty?" She grabbed a beer then headed back towards the couch.

"Yeah, it is. Our honesty, not his. He's helping us out. If he has stuff going on that he doesn't want to talk about, that's his business," Olivia moaned as she followed after Claudia.

Even their bickering was cute. Not full of pain and heartbreak like mine and Aubrey's. *Maybe getting a female's perspective could help me?*

"Yes, that's all well and good, Sweets, but he hasn't told us his plan yet, has he? So, for all we know, he could be gaining all this information for your father."

Olivia gasped and shot me a worried glance. I chuckled and held my hands up in defense, my finger and thumb holding onto the neck of the beer bottle as I walked over towards them. I sat on the couch opposite them and took a swig of my beer before placing it on the table.

"She has a valid point. Look, I'm not a spy for your father, and there is something up with me. In fact, I would really appreciate hearing your opinions on it — get a woman's perspective. If that's okay?"

Olivia's face lit up, you could tell she was the type who liked to fix things, just like my mom. Claudia, on the other hand, was clearly still suspicious of me, but maybe after I told her about Aubrey, she would soften a little. I hoped so anyway, I was getting a little self-conscious with her giving me the stink eye.

"Yes, yes. We would love to help, wouldn't we Claudia?" Olivia practically vibrated with excitement.

"Yeah, sure. Whatevs."

"Well, you don't have to worry Claudia. I'm not after your girl. In fact, I'm in love with someone back home."

"What? Really? Okay, now I'm interested. Spill."

Claudia perked right up. I guess she was worried about me having an ulterior motive, and why wouldn't she? She didn't know me, so why would she trust me with her relationship or their future?

"Her name is Aubrey."

I took my phone out of my pocket and scrolled through the pictures. Although I'd thrown my original phone down the toilet, I'd spent the car ride downloading the pictures of us and her off of my Google drive. I kept telling myself I wanted to move on, but every chance I got to keep a hold of her, I did.

I found a picture of us at the sorority welcome party. It wasn't a loved-up picture, in fact, it was a fake grin from her, one second away from being an eye roll. But that was the night I realized that I was completely in love with her. When I saw Jesse with his hands all over her, it felt like someone had just staked me through the heart. I'd never felt pain like it before. Sure, I wanted her before, but it was more the excitement of the chase and her Scion scent. That night was the night I realized she was my everything, she was my world.

I knew she was my one, the moment I laid eyes on her, but this was more. I wasn't exactly sure when it happened, but the girl well and truly got under my skin. When she ran away with Jesse, I couldn't breathe, it was like all the air had been sucked out of my lungs, and the pain in my chest was excruciating. When Jesse drove away, I collapsed to the floor, and that's when Arabella called my father and uncle.

"Wow, she's so beautiful. You're a very lucky guy," Claudia said with a smile.

"Not so lucky. We broke up." I pulled the phone away and shoved it into my pocket.

"Oh no, what happened?"

"She's in love with my cousin," I answered bluntly and honestly.

"Damn. That's harsh," Claudia said with sympathy.

"Is she with your cousin now?" Olivia asked cautiously.

I shook my head and took a swig of my beer, stalling the next sentence as long as I could.

"He's dead."

"Eww, he's a bloodsucker?" Olivia asked with disgust.

"Either that or she's into necrophilia," Claudia joked before taking a sip of her own beer.

"Claudia!" Olivia snapped, but I couldn't help but laugh. I leaned forward, tilting my beer bottle towards hers. She shot me a wink then clinked her bottle with mine. I had to give her props; it was a good one.

"Nah, see she was in love with him first. Then he died in a car accident."

"Oh my God, Chase. I'm so sorry," Olivia said with a gasp, quickly followed by an apologetic Claudia,

"Damn, dude, I didn't mean ... I'm sorry ... I ..."

"It's okay, honestly. I actually needed that laugh. The whole situation has been nothing but pain and anguish, it's about time I began looking at it a different way. God knows how I've been handling it lately hasn't worked. I went from ignoring it all completely, until I couldn't anymore, then I kicked her out of my car and left."

"Whoa, now that's rough," Claudia stated.

"I know. Look, I'll tell you everything, from beginning to end. Maybe you two can help me, while I help you?"

They looked at each other, then back at me. As their devilish eyes met mine, I wasn't sure if I'd done the right thing. I hoped that they could give me some advice, oh hell, I wished that they'd make the decision for me. God knows I didn't have a clue what I was doing. I loved Aubrey, but I left her. I needed them to either tell me to run to her and beg her to take me back. Or, tell me to keep running in the opposite direction. Sadly, they did neither.

"Now, I have a plan, but this is going to take time. We need to work out if it's just the Scion bond, or if she is truly your one. My dad had to choose between two Scions, and he used a witch to work it out," Olivia rambled on with excitement. I didn't have the heart to interrupt her.

But my mind was going overtime, I didn't really want anyone else involved. If it worked, or at least gave me some sort of answer, I was willing to give it a go. I didn't know how long it would take, but I was willing to try anything at this point. My heart wanted me to run back to Aubrey, and beg for forgiveness, but my head was having none of it. If these women trusted me with the future of their relationship, the least I could do was trust them with mine.

"Also, we can ask the witch to see if there is a way to help Aubrey move on from your cousin. Whether you get back together or not, it's not healthy to pine over a dead man," Claudia interrupted my chain of thought. I agreed with her entirely, even if we didn't manage to rekindle our relationship, the least I owed her was a life of peace.

I knew she wouldn't be happy with me using witches behind her back again, but it really wasn't healthy for her to be so focused on a dead man. She had a right to move on. She had a right to be happy. I knew that she also had a right to grieve in her own time, but she wasn't getting any better. If anything, she was thinking and obsessing about him more with each passing day.

"Okay, let's do this. What do you need me to do?"

They both glanced at each other. Then with wide and unsettling grins, they both looked back at me. I gulped as I thought, *what have I gotten myself into?*

CHAPTER

Six

That night at the hotel we talked for hours, going through plans, throwing ideas out there, and smoothing them out. We made our way back to Olivia's house the next day, after dropping Claudia off with her tribe. We convinced our parents that we wanted a courting period. It wasn't an unusual request; a lot of Scions chose to date a potential mate for a while before making a permanent decision.

Luckily for me, my parents had no reason to suspect anything, and Olivia's were just happy that she was finally showing an interest in a future Alpha. My parents went home, while I was moved into a spare room within the Stonefeather household. Claudia had agreed to stay away for a few weeks at least. In the early stages of this, we couldn't risk any suspicion.

A faint tap on my bedroom door stirred me a little. I groaned and rolled over in bed. It was a few seconds before another tap rapped on the door. This time it was louder and more urgent. I sat up in bed and turned on the light that sat on the bedside table. I glanced at my phone; it was 2 am. A low growl escaped me as I dragged myself out of bed and made my way over to the door.

I opened the door and didn't even get a chance to greet a nervous Olivia. She pushed past me and headed over toward the bed. I quietly closed the door behind me and rubbed my tired eyes.

"What's up Liv?"

"You need to get dressed. I have secured a meeting with the Tintagel triplets, but they can only meet us in an hour. Don't ask me why, they are extremely difficult to pin down."

I got some clothes out, and without thinking pulled my pajama top up and over my head. Olivia blushed and turned away from me with a huff. I chuckled. She wanted me to get dressed, and said we didn't have a lot of time, so what did she expect? I pulled on my t-shirt and slipped out of my bottoms. I could see her squirming and trying her best to avoid looking at me.

Regardless of her love for Claudia, and her being gay, her body still reacted to the fact that I was a future Alpha. I quickly pulled on my pants because I felt a little sorry for her. Being in love with someone so much, but having your body let you down as soon as a future leader came around. Another reason why she needed to get married and be marked by Claudia. All the animal attraction would cease then.

"You can turn around now," I let her know it was safe and I

was covered up. "So, these triplets are the witches you told me about, right?"

"Yeah, they are really powerful, and notoriously difficult to pin down. Luckily for us, they owe my family a favor or two," she said as she turned around to face me. She sat on the bed and continued, "Look, are you sure you want to do this to Aubrey? I mean she won't have a clue that you've done anything at all, but can you live with the fact that you've altered her mind?"

I ran my hand through my hair and with a sigh I replied,

"She won't be happy if she ever finds out. I used witches to wipe her memory before, but I'm not intending for her to find out about this."

I sat on the bed beside her.

"Well, memory wipes are unstable. Unless performed by a powerful Wiccan they very rarely stick."

"Is that not what you're planning on doing?" I asked with curiosity.

"No. The triplets will cast a well-being spell. It will basically calm her thoughts, open up her mind, and help her think more clearly."

"And you think that will be enough?"

"Yeah. From what you told me, she is overcome with grief, confusion, and love for a man that is never coming back. I discussed it with the Tintagels, and we agreed this would be the best bet."

I nodded my head in agreement. I didn't know if it would work. My experience with magic hadn't been all that successful, but I was willing to give it a go. Regardless, if it helped me get

Aubrey back, she deserved to be at peace. Olivia's cell buzzed. She took it out of her pocket, read the text then stood up, shoving it back in her jeans.

"Okay, they're ready for us. Let's go."

I followed silently behind Olivia as she cracked the bedroom door open, and cautiously peeked out into the hall. She glanced back at me and nodded, letting me know the coast was clear. We crept along the hall, freezing for a few seconds every time a floorboard creaked. My heart was pounding, I hoped that her family didn't spot us sneaking around.

We hadn't discussed what we'd say if we were caught sneaking out of the house. To be honest, I thought we would have met the witches during the day. We hadn't discussed a lot of the plan, and I was now regretting not asking her a crapload of questions. I followed her down the stairs and towards the front door. Seconds away from freedom my heart calmed down.

A booming growl startled me, and without realizing it, I grabbed hold of Olivia's arm. I shot my head around, scanning the darkness around us. I expected to see or hear Charles, but all I heard was a whispered chuckle from Olivia.

"Um, you wanna let go, Chase?"

"Huh?" I asked in confusion while looking back at Olivia.

She glanced down at her arm, a tiny arm that my hand was gripping tightly. I quickly realized how hard I was squeezing it and instantly let go. I lifted my hand and rubbed my neck in embarrassment. *She must think I'm a complete wimp.*

"Sorry. I thought it was your father."

"It was," she replied while opening the front door.

"What? Where?" I asked in a whispered panic.

She chuckled and ushered me out of the house. I left the house, hurried down the stairs and onto the drive. I turned back trying to see if I could spot her father, but I couldn't see anything. *Was she joking?*

"My father growls in his sleep. Sometimes he's so loud it wakes the entire house. Now hurry up, they're waiting for us at the end of the drive."

She sprinted off down the path, leaving me staring up at the house. I gulped and shook my head. I hadn't heard a growl that fierce before. I couldn't deny, knowing that I'd dodged a bullet of fighting him to the death, made me feel a little relieved. On the other hand, if he ever found out what we had planned, I had no doubt the man would snap my neck like a twig.

I ran after Olivia and came to a stop in front of a black SUV. The door was open, so I hopped in. As soon as my ass hit the seat, the car sped off. The car ride was silent, the faint breathing of its occupants was all that I could focus on. The windows were tinted beyond belief, and the people within the car refused to look at me.

I felt awkward and raised my eyebrows at Olivia when she met my gaze. She gave me a soft smile, then faced forward again. I had no idea where we were going or what they had planned. I also assumed that these weren't the triplets, well, unless only two of them came to collect us. One guy was driving and one in the passenger seat. I suppose the backs of their heads did look similar. They had the same long black hair.

After about twenty minutes the car came to a stop, the two

guys exited the car, leaving Olivia and me sitting there in silence. Suddenly my door flew open and the guys dragged me out of the car. I growled, letting my anger rise to the surface. My skin took on a brilliant white glow as I began to shift.

"Oh no, you don't!" A woman's voice boomed as she placed her fingers onto my temples and began chanting. Quickly my light faded, and my shifting ceased. I didn't understand what was happening. I tried to call out to Olivia, but no words would come out. The world began to fade, and as it did, I felt the men's tight grip on me loosen.

I fell to my knees when visions of Aubrey consumed my mind. The chanting woman was joined by the two guys, and soon the entire room filled with mystical words. I felt two more sets of hands place themselves onto my shoulders, and as their grip got tighter a sharp pain ripped through my head.

"Calm down Chase. You need to relax so they can access your memories. They need to know everything about Aubrey for this to work," Olivia whispered into my ear.

Calm down? Is she serious?

I couldn't calm down even if I wanted to. Every fiber in my body wanted to fight back, rip those fuckers apart. I couldn't move, but it didn't stop the beast within me from wanting to claw its way to the forefront and carve out their hearts.

CHAPTER
Seven

"Chase? Chase, are you okay?" Olivia's faint voice called out to me.

My head was thumping, like I had a hangover or something. I gradually opened my eyes and tried to sit up, but my body was weak. I barely lifted my head an inch off of the pillow before collapsing back down.

"Hold his head up," a woman's voice ordered. I recognized her from the chanting.

A hand slid under my neck and gently pulled my head up slightly. Someone placed a glass to my lips, and the stench of the liquid made me gag. I tried to pull my head away, but a set of strong hands held my head in place. Another hand pinched my nose closed as the disgusting liquid was poured into my mouth.

I gulped and gagged as the thick sludge slipped down my

throat. Once it was all gone, my head rested back onto the pillow, but it didn't stay there long. I twisted to the side and vomited all over the floor. As I coughed and spluttered, a fresh glass of water came into view.

"Here, drink this, it will wash down the taste," one of the guys insisted.

I took the glass of water and began gulping it down. As soon as it hit my stomach, it made me cough again. I sat up and held out the glass, it wasn't water. The burning that filled my throat and stomach killed off the sickness and disgusting taste, but it left behind an unpleasant fire.

After a few more coughs, another glass was offered to me. I shook my head as I coughed.

"It's just water, I promise," the chanting woman's voice said, as she held the glass closer to me.

I grabbed the glass and drank the water as quickly as I could. The fire began to subside, and the coughing ceased. I placed the glass on the floor and fell back onto the couch. My headache was slowly easing, and my thoughts were becoming clearer. I still didn't have a clue what had happened, but I was glad it was over.

I looked around, and it seemed like we were in an abandoned house of some sort. Candles that were spread around lit the room up slightly, just enough for me to see ripped and dirty wallpaper, flaking paint that was covered by graffiti, and Wiccan symbols drawn all over the place. The couch, thankfully, looked new, as did the pillow and blanket that was next to me.

In a raspy voice, I asked,

"What happened? Why did you attack me?"

The woman laughed, clearly finding my question hilarious. I, on the other hand, was deadly serious. I opened up my eyes and glared at the woman in front of me. I was shocked by her beauty. With caramel skin, dark brown eyes, jet-black hair and a body to die for, she was a goddess for sure.

Beside her stood two large men. You could tell they were related. They had the same dark brown eyes and jet-black hair. The guys were identical, and their facial features looked a lot like the woman's.

I glanced at the woman and her laughter halted.

A smile spread across her face as she replied, "Sorry. We didn't attack you. We needed your mind to be as blank as possible; we couldn't let you know what we were going to do. You did well though, we managed to learn everything about Aubrey, and the spell is complete."

"So, what does that mean? What exactly have you done to her?"

The woman took a seat next to me on the couch. "Basically, she won't be haunted by thoughts of Jesse any longer. We also believe that he is still alive..."

I shot up off of the couch, spun around to face her and snapped, "Impossible. If you'd have seen that wreckage, you would know he was dead. I saw his body with my own two eyes."

One of her brothers cleared his throat from behind me, making her glance up at him. "This isn't our business!"

She raised her eyebrows, before rolling her eyes at him as she replied, "Ugh, fine. It's not my place to disclose other witch's spells. Anyway, Aubrey won't see him anymore, she will gradually think about him less and less, and finally, be able to move on in peace."

I sat back down beside her happy in the knowledge that Aubrey would begin to get her life back, without being consumed with grief. But my mind couldn't help but wonder, *There can't be any truth to what she said, right? I swear I saw his body. Sure, it was beaten up pretty bad, but it was definitely him.*

"Chase, look, there are a lot of things at play here. A whole heap of people entwined with yours and Aubrey's life energies. I'm not sure how this road will turn out for you both, but I do know that she is in some way meant for you. You are a beautiful man, with an honorable soul. Aubrey is very lucky to have your love. Whatever happens, never lose sight of who you are."

"Irene, you ready?" One of her brothers asked her.

She nodded her head and he held his hand out for her. She took his hand and stood up. He placed his hand on the small of her back and guided her over towards the door. Her other brother waited at the door and held it open for her. I watched as they helped her down the stairs, before closing the door behind them.

"Um, so how are we supposed to get home? And why did they look like they were one step away from carrying her out of here?" I asked Olivia as she sat next to me.

"Well, Claudia is on her way to pick us up. And the reason why they guided Irene out, is because she's blind."

I let out a burst of laughter,

"Oh yeah, good one." My laughter faded when Olivia's expression didn't change. "You're being serious?"

She nodded her head with eyebrows raised to her hairline.

"Oh geez, now I feel like an asshole for laughing."

She chuckled and replied, "You weren't to know, she doesn't look blind, and she can actually see people's life energies. She explained it was like a colorful outline of a person. She was quite impressed by yours." She gave me a cheeky wink, and I couldn't help but blush.

We heard a car beep outside.

"Are you ready to get out of here?" Olivia asked as she stood up and held her hand out for me.

"Definitely. I think I could sleep for days."

I took her hand and let her help me up, I was still feeling a little weak, so I appreciated all the help I could get. We headed outside and into Claudia's car. I got into the back of the car and barely remembered sitting down. The next thing I knew, we were back at Olivia's house and I was being escorted to the front door by both girls.

As we neared the porch, the front door flew open.

"Where the hell have you been?" Theia snapped in a raised whisper.

"We thought we'd see how well he could keep up with a Stonefeather boozy night out. Didn't want him embarrassing us at the wedding," Olivia replied.

"Well, that looks like it went swimmingly," Theia said with a chuckle. "Christ, get him up to bed before your father sees him. The poor guy would never live it down."

The girls rushed me into the house. Even though I was feeling better, I made sure to stumble a little as they helped me up the stairs. I couldn't believe that was the first thing that came to her mind. Now I looked like a complete lightweight. Well, it was better than telling her the truth.

The girls helped me into my room, and rather than walking me over to my bed like I thought they would, they both let go of me at the same time. I fell to the floor like a sack of crap and the room erupted with quiet laughter.

"Sorry, Chase, couldn't resist," Claudia mocked.

"Yeah, yeah, very funny," I moaned while dragging myself off the floor.

I stumbled over to my bed and just threw myself onto it face first. I didn't even care that I was still fully clothed. I laid there with my arms spread out, legs half hanging off the edge. I'd never been so comfortable in my life. I heard them leave the room.

Just as I drifted off to sleep, I heard Olivia say, "Goodnight Chase, I hope the spell works and you can win Aubrey back."

CHAPTER
Eight

Six weeks went by and our plan to fool Olivia's parents was going well. They had pretty much adopted me as their son. We had worked out a plan with the Tintagel triplets to be able to get Olivia and Claudia married, without implicating me or my pack. We had a few more meetings scheduled so that we could run over the finer details some more.

Today was one of those meetings. As far as Charles and Theia were aware, Olivia and I were heading off for a romantic long weekend. What we were really doing was going to the triplet's house for the night, then Olivia and Claudia were going away for two days to celebrate their third anniversary. I'd be staying behind at Irene and her brothers' house until the girls got back.

I had already packed my bag and had a shower. I got dressed

and dried my hair. While styling it with some gel there was a tap on the door.

"Come in."

"Oh my God, it smells like you've showered in cologne," she said between coughs while waving her hand around in the air, trying to waft the smell away.

I didn't think I'd put too much on. "You're overreacting, it's not that strong."

"Really? I can barely breathe in here," she complained while pushing open the window. She took in an exaggerated pull of air then slowly let it back out when she turned around to face me.

I rolled my eyes at her while straightening out the collar of my shirt.

"So why are you getting all dressed up?" Olivia asked with a judgmental raised eyebrow, and a half-cocked smirk. While folding her arms, she continued, "it wouldn't be for Irene's benefit, now would it?"

I shook my head and placed my hands into my pocket. Edging towards the door, I replied, "No, of course not. It's our special weekend away, remember? I need your parents to believe that I'd make every effort for my future wife."

I couldn't look at her while spinning the lie. It felt silly. I was in love with Aubrey, but Irene and I had an undeniable connection. It wasn't the animal attraction that I had with Aubrey or the Scion attraction I had towards Olivia. It was something on a different level. It was like Irene and I could be amazing friends. She made me laugh a lot, and she made me feel good about myself.

45

When I spent time with her, my face physically hurt from smiling and laughing so much. We didn't do anything out of the ordinary, just played computer games and watched movies, but every minute with her felt special and extremely natural. We also went hunting together and she was surprisingly good at it considering her lack of eyesight. I found myself regularly staring at her with admiration and awe, she was an incredible person.

Whenever we were together, everything and everyone else faded into the background. With Irene around, as cliché as it sounds, the sun seemed to shine brighter, the birds sang louder and the days were filled with laughter. We didn't take ourselves too seriously and just had fun. Yet, guilt soon consumed me once I was alone. I couldn't help but feel guilty about building a friendship with her.

Regardless of how innocent it may have been, my heart belonged to Aubrey. Although I couldn't deny that I got a kick out of flirting and spending time with Irene. God knows it had been such a long time since I'd felt a connection like that. Aubrey had been so distant the last few months of our relationship and I felt alone the majority of the time.

Olivia shook her head as she walked out of the bedroom door. I guessed she didn't believe me. I picked up my bag and closed the bedroom door behind me. We walked down the stairs and were greeted by Charles and Theia. They hugged their daughter and me, and then wished us a fun weekend. Once the goodbyes had been said, Olivia and I left the house and got into her car. We then drove off towards the Tintagel's.

Olivia was driving and I must have fallen asleep. I was startled awake when she slammed on the brakes while screaming her head off. I couldn't help but spring up in my seat and begin screaming too. Her screams turned into a hysterical fit of laughter long before the feminine squeal ceased from my own lips.

I turned towards her, heart-pounding, beads of sweat pouring down my face and a sore throat from screaming so loud. I furrowed my brow at her while yelling, "What the fuck was that?"

"That was you screaming like a little bitch. That's what that was," she replied in short bursts between chuckles.

"Yes, I'm aware of that. Why did you break and scream like that?"

"Because we're here, and I thought it would be funny," she said again in between chuckles, "and Olivia was completely right. It was hilarious."

"Okay. Okay. You've had your fun. For that, you can carry the bags."

I got out of the car and slammed the door behind me, then stomped up the path towards the house. I could hear her muttering behind me, "that was so worth it." I reached the door and rang the bell. It was quickly opened by one of Irene's brothers.

"Idris?" I asked while holding my hand out.

He took my hand and shook it while replying, "Ivan actually, but hey, how are you doing?"

"Damn. One of these days I'll be able to tell you two apart," I replied with a nervous laugh escaping my lips.

"It's okay, even our coven struggled to tell us apart," Idris shouted out as he made his way over to greet me.

He shook my hand and pulled me in for a hug. It was so nice being there, it felt like a home away from home. The guys began laughing as they looked behind me, so I turned to see what was going on. Halfway down the drive was a tiny Olivia struggling with two large bags and a pull along suitcase. She looked so ridiculous, I couldn't help but giggle.

"Oh no, it's okay guys. I'm fine carrying this stuff all by myself. I don't need any help or anything," she cried out sarcastically, as she leaned forward even more from the weight of the bags. The poor thing looked like an old lady.

The guys laughed again, then pushed past me to go and help her. Idris took the two bags and Ivan pulled along the suitcase. Olivia stood up straight holding onto her lower back as she leaned back to stretch it out. She then proceeded to storm towards the door and shouted out to the guys as she walked by me.

"Thank you, guys. I'm glad there are still some gentlemen left in this world." She shot me a glare as she entered the house, and I couldn't help but crack up.

I looked over to the guys, their cheeky grins making me laugh all the more. I finished my giggling, making sure I was composed as I walked into the house. Sitting down next to Olivia, mainly to piss her off some more, we waited for the guys to join us. They put our bags in a room down the hall then disappeared. When Idris returned, he handed me and Olivia an open beer each, then sat on the couch opposite us.

"So, um where's Irene?" I asked casually before quickly taking a sip of my beer.

Olivia took a sideways glance at me then rolled her eyes. I

ignored her judgments. I was just curious. There was nothing behind the question.

Ivan entered the room and shook his head at his brother. They exchanged a few weird looks before Ivan said, "Irene hasn't been feeling well the last few days, so she's hiding out in her room. She doesn't want to make anyone sick."

He sat down next to his brother and began drinking his beer. I stood up and turned towards the hallway.

"Oh no, should I go and see her? Check if she needs anything?" I asked while looking down the hall and pointing a finger in that direction.

"No!" Idris snapped in a panicked voice. He took a deep breath then continued, "she's fine, it's just a tiny curse. We are used to them, but your kind wouldn't be."

"Okay. Um, well I hope she feels better soon," I replied as I took my seat again.

"Yeah, she'll be fine in a few days, don't worry yourself."

I furrowed my brow and shot a confused look at Olivia. I could tell by her face she was suspicious too, but she just shrugged as she took a sip of her drink. The guys asked Olivia what she wanted to order for dinner, so she went and joined them on their couch to look through the menu.

I crossed one leg over the other and placed my arm over the back of the couch. I relaxed for a little bit while the others decided what food to order, but I couldn't stop thinking about Irene. The guys were definitely hiding something. I drank my beer and stared down the dimly lit hallway as I thought, *I wonder what's really wrong with her?*

49

CHAPTER Nine

After drinking way too much beer, eating way too much pizza, and watching a bunch of crappy horror films, I'd finally crawled down the hall towards my room. Olivia had gone to bed upstairs hours ago, but I and the guys stayed up. I must have fallen asleep at some point, and when I woke my body was aching from the strange position I'd fallen asleep in.

Leaving the guys sleeping in the living room, I continued to make my way down the hall. As my hand grabbed hold of the door handle to my room a delicious and irresistible scent hit my nose. A growl began to rumble in my chest as my hand squeezed tightly around the door handle. I frantically sniffed at the air, and as I turned to follow it, I ripped the door handle clean off of the door.

The noise must have awoken the guys because when I began to sprint towards a door at the end of the hall, I heard chanting behind me. I took no notice and picked up my speed. I needed to get to that scent. It was like my body had been taken over, I had no control over what it was doing. All I was focused on was that aroma. The chanting behind me grew louder and as it did, I heard Olivia scream.

I reached the door, which was concealing the scent, it was weak, but it was there. I guessed a spell had been used to cover up the smell, but it hadn't worked entirely. My hand stretched out to clasp the door handle but as I did the guys' chanting got louder and I found myself hurtling through the air. I was slammed into the wall, and as I lay crumpled on the floor, the guys walked closer to me.

I was unable to move my body at all. Their chanting had me pinned down, light green sparks and lights flowed out of their fingers and floated around me like vines. I couldn't control my wolf, he wanted out, and I couldn't understand why. But as soon as Irene opened her bedroom door and stepped out, it all became clear. Her scent hit me like a freight train.

"You're in heat?" I snarled at her.

She nodded her head at me but said nothing.

"What? How is that even possible?" Olivia asked, in a voice that carried the same shock that I felt.

She didn't bother to answer Olivia either, she just made her way towards me, clutching hold of a glass filled with some sort of thick green liquid. I tried to squirm but couldn't.

"Don't come near me, Irene. Please, I can't control my wolf," I begged her.

She ignored my pleas and crouched down in front of me. She held the glass to my lips and made me drink the disgusting concoction. Coughing and spluttering caused me to collapse to the ground and before I knew it the world turned black as I passed out.

When I awoke, I was strapped down to a bed in my room while Irene sat next to me. With blurry eyes, I tried to look at her. I could see her outline, but with a few more blinks she finally came into focus.

"What happened? Why am I tied down?" I asked while pulling at my leather restraints.

"The potion I gave you knocks out your sense of smell, but the guys wanted you tied down just in case."

"That's fair, I guess."

I let my head fall onto the pillow as she began to talk again.

"Clearly your wolf is very strong. You shouldn't have been able to smell me through the ward on my bedroom door, but you could. I don't understand why," she said with genuine confusion.

"Well, I don't understand any of this. How can you be a witch and a werewolf? It's impossible."

"Not impossible, but extremely rare," she corrected.

"I've never heard of such a thing. How didn't I smell it before?" I asked while turning my head to look at her.

"Well, I had a cloaking spell on me and my brothers. We don't like to advertise what we are."

"That's understandable. There would be a lot of interest in your kind."

"There would. That is why I'm begging you not to say anything to anyone. Please, Chase, no one can know what we are," she took my hand into hers as she begged me to keep their secret.

"Of course, Irene. I won't tell anyone. I swear to you, I'd never put you or your brothers in danger like that."

She smiled widely as she let out a breath of relief. She lowered her head, and I could see a tear slide down her cheek as her emotion took over. I reached my hand up, but it soon got stopped by the leather strap. I began to lower it back down, when she grabbed a hold of the strap and untied it. My hand shot up and cupped her face.

She purred as my thumb swept across her cheek, wiping away the stray tear. My heart swelled when she rubbed her face on my hand. Her cheek was so soft, and as I stared at her beautiful plump lips, all I wanted to do was rip these restraints off and kiss her. Seeming to sense my intentions, she gently pulled my hand away from her face and secured it again with the leather strap.

"Look, I'm in the last throes of my heat. It should be over by morning. I'll come and find you, and we can discuss everything. Okay?"

I nodded my head in agreement. Anything she told me right now wouldn't sink in completely. My sense of smell was beginning to return already, and I could feel my wolf starting to stir. She stood up and reached for a glass on the side.

"Left a little," I instructed.

Her hand moved to the left, bumping gently into the glass. She picked it up and fed me the gross green drink again. I tried my best to hold back my gag reflex as the thick goo ran down the back of my throat.

After coughing a little, I said, "Can't you come up with a potion that doesn't taste like ass?"

She giggled while shaking her head. "Goodnight, Chase."

"Goodnight, Irene."

I slept well that night. I'm not sure if it was exhaustion or if Irene had fed me more potion in the night, but I woke feeling refreshed. My restraints were gone, so I was able to enjoy a much-needed stretch. I had a lot of questions for Irene and the guys. I'd never heard of witch-werewolves before, and the idea fascinated me. It would totally explain the unusual connection I have to Irene and her brothers. They felt like family, and now I knew why.

I could smell again, and the scent of freshly cooked bacon had my stomach growling. I ate a lot last night, and with the amount I drank, I was surprised I didn't have a hangover. *Maybe the potion made me hungry and is an amazing hangover cure?* I thought as I got out of bed and headed out of my bedroom. I followed the smell towards the dining room.

Once I reached the dining-room door, I could hear chatting. It sounded like everyone was awake. I stood there for a second and tried to listen in, but as I edged my ear closer to the door, it suddenly opened, making me jump. An amused Idris or Ivan, I wasn't quite sure, was standing there with a huge grin on his face. I straightened up and smiled back awkwardly.

"Werewolf senses remember?"

"I was hoping it was all a dream," I lied casually as I strolled into the room and took a seat at the dining table.

"Yeah, sure you were," he replied sarcastically, pulling a chuckle from Olivia.

I scowled at her, making her bow her head and continue to eat her breakfast. I wanted answers to the hundreds of questions I had racing through my mind, but the bacon, sausages, mushrooms and waffles smelled so delicious, I couldn't resist. I began to dig into my food and decided the questions could wait.

Whatever was in that drink had me feeling ravenous, or it could have been the fact that I had been in such close proximity to a she-wolf in heat. In our packs, we always had the wolves in heat locked away, far from the reaches of any male werewolf. It had been like that for so long that none of the males knew what it was like to be around a wolf in heat unless it was their mates.

I finished off my breakfast in record time, and the guys poked fun at me for stuffing my face so fast. It was delicious. I also wanted it finished quickly so I could begin asking questions. The last mouthful of my food was barely swallowed before I spat out the first question.

"So, you're a litter? Does that mean your mother is a werewolf?"

CHAPTER
Ten

I spent all day asking Irene questions. Her brothers had long given up and headed to bed, and Olivia had left for her weekend with Claudia. It was just me and Irene, and I couldn't deny that it felt so natural being around her. We'd ordered some food, eaten it, and were now sitting on the couch together having a drink.

The triplets' story was a dark one, to say the least. Irene explained that her mom was a young werewolf who had been kidnapped by a black magic coven. They were the worst of the worst in the magic community and kept themselves well hidden. They had a prophecy that said if they were able to impregnate a werewolf that was the seventh daughter of the seventh son, they would bring forth a litter of the strongest witches the world had ever seen.

Needless to say, their plan worked, and Irene's mom was soon pregnant. She went through the beginning of the pregnancy held captive by the coven, but then managed to escape. She found the protection of a white witch coven, who welcomed her with open arms, cloaked her from the world, and kept her safe until the end of her pregnancy. Sadly, she passed away shortly after delivering Irene and her brothers. The children were raised by the white witches, but as their powers began to emerge, the black coven found out where they were being held.

The black coven killed large amounts of Irene's coven in search of the triplets. Irene decided to try a powerful cloaking spell. The triplets' powers were new and highly volatile. Although the spell worked and hid them out of sight from the magical community, it sadly had irreversible consequences and that's how Irene lost her sight.

The life that Irene, Idris and Ivan had to endure was like that out of a storybook. I couldn't believe that they had been through all of that and had turned out to be such amazing people. They were so kind and always tried to help others. If I had been through all that, I doubted I would have turned out as well adjusted as they had.

It was late in the night and I could tell that Irene was exhausted. After going through her heat, and then answering all of my questions all day, I was surprised she was still awake. I took a sip of my beer as I watched her yawn, covering her mouth with her delicate hand.

"Excuse me. That's so rude of me," she quickly apologized.

"Of course, it isn't. Your body has been through a lot, and I've selfishly kept you up all night. I'm the one who should be apologizing."

"It's fine, Chase, honestly. I can understand your curiosity. It's not every day you meet werewolf witches, now is it?" she said with a chuckle.

"No, it's not, but I should have let you go to bed hours ago. Shall I walk you to your room?" I asked while placing my beer on the table.

I began to stand up but stopped when her hand gently grabbed my arm. I sat back onto the couch and stared into her eyes. It was a strange feeling, knowing that I was looking into her eyes, and although hers were gazing right back, she couldn't see me. It was as though I was staring deep into her soul, and it scared the crap out of me. It made me feel a kind of love for her that I shouldn't have been feeling.

"I can make my own way there. I'm afraid if you escort me to my room, I won't be able to control my actions," she said with a serious expression. I cleared my throat and was going to say something, but she continued before I had the chance. "I wish we'd met under different circumstances, Chase. I know how happy we could have been together, but as a future Alpha, you deserve a Scion. You will make a fantastic father, and I couldn't take that away from you."

She got up and headed off down the hall. I sat back down and ran both my hands through my hair as I exhaled. A light chuckle left my lips as my head shook from side to side. I couldn't believe she had been so forward. Not that I could deny the feelings I had towards her. They were definitely there. She was right. I had a duty to my pack to carry on our line. The only way I could do that was with a Scion; with Aubrey.

After finishing my beer, I headed off to my room. I stripped down to my boxers and got into bed. Laying there in the dark, I tried to sleep, but thoughts and visions of Aubrey and Irene swam through my mind. I wondered what my future would be like with Irene — she was kind, compassionate and selfless. Then I wondered what my future held with Aubrey — she was fun, sweet, and a Scion.

I let out an exaggerated sigh while turning over in bed, trying to get more comfortable. I loved Aubrey so much, *but will she ever love me the way she loves Jesse? I need to see her. I need to see if the spell has worked. I want answers. Can I go back to Murston and pick up where I left off? Or has too much happened? Will she even want me back? And will I be able to stop thinking about Irene?*

I'm not exactly sure if I gave myself any answers to those questions, because I must have fallen asleep shortly after asking them. I woke up to the sound of the birds chirping outside, and surprisingly I didn't have a headache for a change. I actually felt quite refreshed, better than I'd felt in ages. I got out of bed and went to take a shower. After showering I got dressed and headed out into the kitchen.

Idris was cooking breakfast--bacon, eggs and pancakes by the smell of it. I sat down at the dining table and said, "That smells delicious."

"Thanks. You want some coffee to go with it?"

"Yeah sure. That would be great, thanks."

He poured out two coffees and brought them over to the

table, then went back and piled a bunch of food onto two plates. He strolled back over and placed a plate in front of me and one opposite me, then sat down. I looked around the room, wondering if Ivan and Irene would be joining us, but I couldn't smell or hear anyone else in the house. Idris didn't wait for anyone either and quickly began tucking into his huge plate of food.

"Not eating?" he asked with a mouthful of food while pointing to my plate with his fork.

"I was waiting for Ivan and Irene."

"Oh, they're not here. Irene needed some space, so Ivan took her to a close friend's house," he said before shoving another filled fork of food into his mouth.

"Is it because of me?" I asked curiously while picking up my own knife and fork.

A grunt and a head nod were all I got in reply.

"I'm sorry if I made things awkward. I should leave," I said while placing my cutlery down on the table.

"No, dude. Sit. Eat. It's Irene that made it awkward. She knows you're off-limits. You're a future Alpha, and not to mention you're already in love with a Scion. She insisted on leaving for the weekend."

He held his fork out, inviting me to sit again. I started eating my breakfast and as the minutes passed, I thought less and less about Irene. I guessed she had performed the same spell on me that she had for Aubrey. It wasn't that I didn't still have feelings for her, it was just I was content with the situation, and wasn't bombarded with feelings or thoughts of her.

"Ivan will be back soon, and we can go over the plans for the wedding," Idris stated as he finished off the last bite of his breakfast.

"Okay, cool. We need to get it all planned out."

"Yeah, the sooner we have all the details figured out, the sooner you can go home and get your Scion."

That thought brought a smile to my face. It had been ages since I'd seen or spoken to Aubrey, but I was still a little apprehensive. I didn't know whether or not she'd even want me back. I hadn't spoken to anyone really — at least I hadn't bothered to ask about her. I didn't know if she'd moved on or how she was doing, and although that made me feel guilty, I couldn't hear about her. I couldn't handle knowing if she was doing bad or good.

We finished breakfast, and soon enough Ivan arrived. We spent the weekend going over the plans, checking and double-checking, making sure that nothing could go wrong. By the time Olivia and Claudia got back, we had everything ironed out, and filled them in on what was going to happen.

Over the next few months we went over the plans a few more times, and spent time convincing our parents that we were a proper couple. The whole time I couldn't keep Aubrey from my thoughts and it eventually became unbearable. So when we finally booked a date for the wedding and told my parents that we planned on getting married in Murston, I was beyond ecstatic to be going home.

It had been nearly six months and I didn't know how Aubrey was going to feel. Olivia had told me to contact Brie before showing up but I still wasn't sure if she wanted to see me or even wanted me back. So I decided to just head home and see how she reacted to me. I contacted Bear and Connor to let them know that I was coming home with Olivia. They insisted on throwing me a welcome back party.

It wasn't what I wanted, but they'd missed me, so I couldn't deny them a bit of a celebration. Although I did insist that they keep Aubrey away from the party. Even though I wanted to see her as soon as I could, rocking up with a new fiancé wouldn't exactly set the tone I was going for. I needed the pack to believe I found a new Scion, and that we were in love and due to be married. But I had to explain it all to Aubrey before she saw Olivia.

"Are you looking forward to going home?" Olivia asked as she entered my room.

While packing my bag I replied, "Yeah, I'm super excited. It's been a long time." Those were the words that came out of my mouth, but in my mind, I was freaking out.

What if Aubrey doesn't want me? What if she's moved on? Oh my God, what if this all goes wrong? Olivia's dad will kill me!

With my heart pounding, sweat beading above my brow, I took in a deep breath as I zipped up my bag and threw it over my shoulder. I placed my arm around Olivia's waist and said, "Let's go marry our girls!"

THE END

A very special thank you to
Tonya Cueto
Jon-G Jimenez
Andreea Pryde
Jennifer Danielle

For helping me to pick out names for this book, and for your continued interaction on my Facebook group. I really wouldn't be able to do it without all you amazing ladies.

Thank you to Tre & Shannon for proofreading this for me, you ladies are the best, love ya. Xoxo

Captured By The Night is the next book in the first duet of the Scion series, the link for its pre-order is below.

If you would like to follow me and check out my other stories then follow the links below. Thank you for reading my book, please leave a review if you could xoxo

Pre-Order Links

Captured By The Night

The Freya Rose Series

Adored By An Alpha

Abandoned By An Alpha Audiobook

Honored By A Hunter

Heartbroken By A Hunter

Saved By A Sire King

Standalone Books

An Alpha For Dahlia

Follow Me

You can follow me on the below links:

Amazon: @L-P-Dillon
Facebook: @L.P. Dillon
Facebook Page: @AuthorL.P.Dillon
Facebook Group: @Author L.P.Dillon's Divas
Bookbub: @l-p-dillon
GoodReads: @L.P. Dillon
Twitter: AuthorLPDillon
Instagram: @l.p.dillon
TikTok: @@l.p.dillon

See you all in August for the final book in Aubrey, Chase and Jesse's story.

L.P.Dillon
xoxo

Made in the USA
Middletown, DE
01 July 2023

34268401R00047